DANGER IN THE OUTLANDS

Scholastic Inc.

"The Mirror Trees," "In the Lair of Lavertus," and "A Web of Wood" written by Greg Farshtey.

Illustrated by Ameet Studio

ISBN 978-0-545-62788-7

LEGO, the LEGO logo, the Brick and Knob configurations, the Minifigure and LEGENDS OF CHIMA are trademarks of the LEGO Group. ©2014 The LEGO Group. Produced by Scholastic Inc. under license from the LEGO Group.

Published by Scholastic Inc. SCHOLASTIC and associated logos are trademarks and/or registered trademarks of Scholastic Inc.

10 9 8 7 6 5 4 3 2 1   14 15 16 17 18 19/0

Printed in the U.S.A.   40

First Scholastic printing, May 2014

MIX
Paper from
responsible sources
FSC™ C020056

TABLE OF CONTENTS

A NEW THREAT

My name is Laval. I am the prince of the Lion Tribe. Not long ago, all of the tribes in Chima were fighting for control of the CHI, our most precious energy source. But then, something unexpected happened.

A mysterious black cloud from the Outlands came and surrounded Mount Cavora, the source of all our CHI. When the black cloud vanished, the CHI waterfalls had dried up. We were left with nothing. And without CHI, Chima would perish!

My father, King LaGravis, and the other tribe leaders realized that we needed to stop fighting one another and unite against this new threat. Even though we had our differences, the only way to save Chima was to work together!

UNITED FOR CHIMA

According to the Great Story, our ancestors, the Legend Beasts, would return to save Chima if it was ever threatened. But when the falls of Mount Cavora dried up, the Legend Beasts never came.

We discovered that they had been captured by mysterious new enemies in the Outlands. The same enemies who sent the black cloud to attack Mount Cavora were holding the Legend Beasts prisoner.

Our tribes decided to launch a rescue mission. We each chose one member to go on a quest to the Outlands. I am going on behalf of the Lions, along with Cragger the Crocodile, Eris the Eagle, Worriz the Wolf, Gorzan the Gorilla, Razar the Raven, Rogon the Rhino, and Bladvic the Bear.

Together, we must find the Legend Beasts and bring them back. They are the only ones who can restart Mount Cavora's CHI Falls and restore Chima.

LAVAL SAYS:

Cragger's mother, Queen Crunket, told us the Legend Beasts had been captured. She escaped from the Outlands on the Crocodile Legend Beast. Now we must save the other seven before it's too late!

THE SCORPIONS

The moment we began our quest in the Outlands, we discovered three new tribes were waiting to battle us: the Scorpions, Spiders, and Bats. These twisted, CHI-hungry creatures were unlike anything we'd ever seen before!

The Scorpions are by far the most powerful of the three new tribes. They are leading the assault on Chima and have enlisted the Spiders and Bats to help them on their crazed mission to conquer us all and control the CHI. Their home base is the Scorpion Cave: a collection of twisting underground tunnels and treacherous caverns.

The Scorpions are vicious warriors: fast, fierce, and equipped with powerful tails that they use for clubbing and stinging. Worse, their tails contain toxic venom. If a Scorpion stings you, its venom will allow it to control your mind for a short while.

Scorm is the Scorpion Tribe's evil king. He is bent on one thing and one thing alone: complete domination. He is obsessed with controlling all of the CHI and making everyone in Chima bow before him.

LAVAL SAYS:

Not only is Scorm power-hungry, but he's also incredibly obnoxious. Everyone in his tribe listens to him because it's easier than disagreeing with him.

THE BATS

I t didn't take long before we discovered the source of the mysterious black cloud that shrouded Mount Cavora. It was the Bats! There are more Bats than any other creature in the Outlands. They can emit a kind of smokescreen from their wings while traveling together, forming a black cloud.

If the Scorpions are the leaders of this new assault, then the Bats are their minions. They are the weakest and dumbest of the Outland Tribes, but they attack in such large numbers that they can be just as deadly. They will often charge first and strategize later, blindly throwing themselves at an enemy until they find a weakness. That's how they penetrated the energy field around Mount Cavora. They just kept flinging themselves at the floating mountain until they found a way in through the waterfalls.

The Bats have flying machines, too, called Bat Flyers. They are small, speedy aircrafts with powerful blasters and "grabber wings" that can pick up warriors. Since the Bats are the only tribe in the Outlands that can fly, they use their flyers to transport Scorpions and Spiders to Mount Cavora to steal CHI.

THE SPIDERS

The Spiders are the cleverest Outland Tribe. They're master engineers by nature and use webs to build cunning traps. A Spider can even shoot its web during battle to tangle up an opponent. This is especially frustrating for Eris and Razar, because it means they're not even safe in the sky.

Spiders are tough warriors, too. They attack with split-second jumps and short, sharp jabs rather than big, roundhouse swings.

All Spiders have eight eyes. They don't understand how other creatures with only two eyes can see. But ironically, the Spiders usually keep their eyes (all eight of them) trained on their queen, Spinlyn. She is the ugliest creature in Chima, yet she believes her beauty is stunning. She wants CHI because she thinks it will make her even more "beautiful." The Spiders' loyal affection for their vain queen is the only reason they all crave CHI.

LAVERTUS

With all the enemies waiting for us in the Outlands, none of us expected to meet a friendly soul on our quest. That was, until we came across Lavertus: a Lion who was exiled from our tribe long ago. I was too young to remember why he was banished, and he won't tell us what happened, either. But given the situation, we're just happy to have a friend in the Outlands we can trust. At least, as far as we know . . .

Lavertus lives in a bizarre mini-fortress he calls his "Lair." There are winding tunnels and doors that lead to nowhere throughout it. But he offered us shelter there all the same, and he even upgraded our weapons and armor. He's a talented inventor and a great warrior.

Lavertus managed to survive for years in the Outlands, but the isolation has made him *very* kooky. He can be pretty moody and strangely secretive. He also seems to like messing with Cragger for some reason. We're not quite sure if he is completely sane. But with the mission ahead of us, my friends and I will take all the help we can get.

TURN THE PAGE FOR THREE EXCITING LEGENDS OF CHIMA™ STORIES!

THE MIRROR TREES

"**R**un!" yelled Rogon the Rhino as he charged down the narrow jungle path.

The eight Chima warriors ran and flew down the trail, flanked on either side by the strange plant life of the Outlands. Behind them a swarm of Bats filled the sky, their leather-like wings flapping and their shrieks piercing the air. Now and then, a handful of the Bats would dive, forcing the heroes to duck for cover.

When the Bats had first appeared, Eris and a reluctant Razar had flown up to try and drive them off. But there were dozens and dozens of the new enemies to contend with, and the Eagle and Raven were quickly forced back.

"Look for a cave we can hide in," said Bladvic the Bear. He was a big fan of caves, since they were dark and cool and great for sleeping.

"Bats love caves," Eris reminded him. "We would be trapped in there."

Worriz ducked as a Bat's spear flew past him. "What if we split up and scatter?" he suggested. "We might be able to confuse them long enough to get away."

"There are too many of them, my friend," said Razar. "Even divided, there would be ten bats for each one of us."

"He's right," said Eris. "We can't beat them with the normal tactics. We need a new strategy, or a new weapon, or faster wings and feet!"

"That's your brilliant plan?" Cragger grumbled as he jumped over a snapping Predator Plant's jaws. "'Run faster'? I thought Eagles were supposed to be experts at coming up with strategies."

"We are!" insisted Eris. "Just not while under attack."

"Guys, there's no time for arguing!" Laval exclaimed. "We have to do something before those Bats chase us off a cliff!"

Rogon tore through some bushes, the others close behind. Just ahead of them was a small clearing with a grove of trees. But the closer the heroes got, the more they realized that the trees were . . . unusual. They were rather short and had shiny, silver leaves that seemed to be made of metal. And the leaves were cupped so that they looked like upside-down bowls.

"Let's get under those trees," cried Laval. "Maybe they will give us some protection."

The eight heroes took cover. Gorzan examined one of the leaves and was amazed to find that he could see his reflection in it.

"Hey," he exclaimed. "I can see myself. Groovy!"

"So can I," said Razar, running a clawed hand through his feathers. "And I look *goooood*."

"They're coming," Laval interrupted. "Get ready."

"They're coming, get ready, they're coming, get ready, they're coming, get ready . . ."

"We heard you the first time!" Cragger snapped.

"That wasn't me," said Laval. "Those are echoes, but I don't know where they're coming from."

Laval looked up through some of the branches on the shiny tree. Yes, the black cloud of Bats was heading their way. Then, right before his eyes, something strange happened. The Bats dove toward the trees in a tight

formation, but as they got close, they started flying in crazy patterns and doing loops.

Over the next few minutes, each Bat attack ended the same way: Just before the Bats reached the treetops, they would start acting confused and scatter.

"What's going on here?" asked Cragger, his words echoing all around. "They're acting like they have been out in the sun too long."

"I don't know," said Laval. "It doesn't make any sense. First, they're chasing us, and then as soon as we went under these trees—"

"Yeah, the trees," said Razar, his eyes on the leaves. "Maybe they don't like seeing themselves in these little mirrors, yes? They have faces even a mother Bat wouldn't love."

High above, the Bats were shrieking in what sounded like anger. Razar cocked his head and said, "Wait a second. Bats don't see well, do they? So they couldn't see themselves in the leaves, no matter how ugly they are."

"That's right!" Eris cried excitedly. "Bats don't rely on their eyes—they use *sonar* to find their way around."

"Sonar?" asked Cragger. "What's that?"

"The Bats are using sound waves as their 'eyes,'" Eris explained. "When they cry out, the sounds bounce off objects so they can tell where things are."

"Of course," said Laval. "If the leaves are bouncing the Bats' cries around the same way they made our voices echo, it could be making their sonar 'blind'!"

Eris looked up through the branches. High above, the Bats were getting ready for another attack. "I have an idea," she said. "Everyone grab as many leaves as you can."

"What good will that do?" asked Worriz.

"Just trust me," Eris insisted, handing out the shiny leaves to her friends. "All set?" she asked. "Now, run—and throw those leaves!"

The eight heroes dashed out from beneath the trees. Immediately, the Bats went into a dive. But before they could reach their targets, Eris and the others started

throwing the leaves high into the air until it looked like a silver rainstorm going from the ground up to the sky.

Already too close, the Bats suddenly found themselves with no idea where to go as the cloud of leaves messed up their sonar. Bats collided with one another, slammed into trees, and some even flew upside down as the leaves fluttered down to the ground. By the time the Bats could "see" again, Laval and the others were long gone.

Once the friends were out of danger, they stopped to catch their breath.

"*Whew,*" said Gorzan. "I guess that's one time the strange things in the Outlands helped us. Good thing those groovy trees were there."

"Yeah." Laval nodded. "And it's a good thing Eris figured out what to do with those leaves, otherwise we might have been stuck there forever. Looks like Eagles *are* the masters of strategy after all, huh, Cragger?"

Cragger grumbled but then nodded his head in agreement. "Yeah, I guess you're right."

Eris smiled. "Thanks. But, it looks like my plan didn't just work at distracting the Bats." She pointed toward Razar. The Raven was holding up one of the mirror leaves, staring at his reflection in the shiny surface.

Eris giggled. "I think those leaves have a secret power over Ravens, too."

"What can I say, my friend?" Razar grinned at his reflection. "If I'm looking good, I'm looking *good*."

IN THE LAIR OF LAVERTUS

"I can't sleep," said Cragger.

Laval rolled over on his sleep mat and peered at the Crocodile through half-closed eyes. "Do what you always do. Count swamp sheep."

"Tried that," said Cragger. "I also tried singing Crocodile lullabies to myself."

"Crocodiles have lullabies?" Laval asked.

"Sure," said Cragger. "They're mostly about what we're going to eat the next day."

"That sounds . . . relaxing, I guess," said Laval. "So why can't you sleep?"

"I don't think I like this place," answered Cragger. "Or maybe I just don't trust our host."

Laval, Cragger, and their friends were on a quest to free the Legend Beasts and restore the flow of CHI from Mount Cavora. On their journey through the mysterious Outlands they had encountered Lavertus, a very odd Lion who lived in a fortress he called his "Lair." He had offered

the team to stay there and use it as a base, as long as they didn't go wandering around after dark.

Cragger got to his feet. "I'm going to take a look around. I think this Lion is up to something."

"None of us should go wandering," Laval warned. "Lavertus told us it isn't safe, and that, at least, I believe."

"I know, I know, Lions *love* following rules," Cragger said, heading for the door. "Well, Crocs make their own."

Laval went after him. "And we all remember what happened because of that. Sometimes, I think you break rules just for the sake of breaking them. Fine—if you're going, I'm going with you."

"Why?" Cragger asked.

"To make sure you don't mess things up . . . again," said Laval.

"Come on, we're on the same side now. You can trust me." Cragger flashed a toothy grin before turning away.

"I used to," muttered Laval, following after him.

It was easy to see that Lavertus's home was designed to make sure any stranger would rapidly get lost inside. Hallways looped around on themselves, doors led to solid

walls, and staircases that went up somehow managed to leave you on a lower floor.

"I've never seen anything like this," whispered Cragger.

"I wish I wasn't seeing it now," answered Laval. "What do you expect to find, anyway?"

"I don't know," said Cragger. "Nobody builds a house like this unless they have something to hide."

"Or they had the directions upside down," Laval said, shaking his head.

The two moved on. After another half hour of searching,

they came upon a corridor lined with doorways on both sides. One by one, they opened the doors.

"Closet. Closet. Closet," said Laval.

"Staircase!" cried Cragger.

Laval rushed over to see what the Crocodile had found. But when he got there, Cragger was standing at an open door looking into another closet.

"Where are the stairs?" asked Laval.

"They were here a second ago," said Cragger, shutting the door. "Then they weren't."

"*Hmmm.* Try opening the door again," said Laval.

Cragger opened the door a second time. When he did, the staircase was back. "That's weird," said the Crocodile. "Let's go see what's down there."

"Got any breadcrumbs?" asked Laval.

"Huh?" snapped Cragger.

"To leave a trail to find our way back," said Laval. "What happens if the stairs disappear again when we're halfway down?"

"Good question," said Cragger. After a short pause, he added, "You go first."

"Right," said Laval. "Because turning my back on you is my favorite thing to do. . . . *Not.*"

The pair stumbled down the staircase side by side. At the bottom, they found an iron door. To their surprise, it was unlocked.

"He must not have thought anyone would find this spot," said Laval.

"Or maybe he wanted whoever did find it to be able to get in, because he knew they wouldn't get back out again," answered Cragger. "You go first."

"Wait a second!" said Laval, turning around to face the Crocodile. "This whole thing was your idea! Why do I have to keep going first?"

"Um, because you're such a fierce fighter and you can handle whatever comes at us?"

Laval glared at Cragger. "Yeah, I'm fierce," he said.

"You might want to remember that if you have any tricks planned. Anyway, I'll go first, because we're supposed to be friends . . . and that's what friends do."

The Lion pushed the door open, even as Cragger said, "Tricks? Me?"

"Yes, you. Just because we're on the same side again doesn't mean—"

Laval stopped short and his eyes grew wide. He and Cragger had stumbled upon the biggest workshop either had ever seen. It was packed with strange devices, big and small. Some were incredibly complicated and others were extremely simple. At a glance, the only things Laval recognized were Speedor wheels and other parts of a Speedor bike.

"Incredible," said Laval. "Eris would love this!"

"If Lavertus made all this, he must be some kind of inventor," said Cragger. "But he didn't tell us. Why keep that a secret?"

"I don't know," answered Laval. "But look at this stuff. Some of it looks like weapons. It could be dangerous. We'd better tell the others."

Just as Laval was speaking, the floor shifted underneath them. The Lion and Croc were knocked off their feet.

"Whoa!" said Laval. "What was that?"

"Laval, look!" cried Cragger, pointing at the iron door. "The stairs are gone!"

Cragger was right. The doorway leading to the stairs now led to a solid wall.

"We're trapped!" Laval realized.

"No, we're not," Cragger said, racing into the heart of the workshop. "There has to be something in here that can get us out."

"Cragger, don't!" Laval cried.

But it was too late. Cragger had bumped into one of Lavertus's inventions: a big metal cannon. It immediately shot out a tangle of ropes that wrapped around him. Cragger toppled backward, falling into a stone chair. The arms of the chair closed tight on either side of the Crocodile and held him fast.

"Hang on," shouted Laval. "I'll get you out."

But as he raced toward Cragger, the floor rumbled again. A small catapult on top of a tall shelf went off, launching a little rock at the head of a life-size Gorilla statue. The statue sprang to life, plodding forward and knocking into more inventions as it went. Soon, the air was filled with arrows, jets of flame, and bursts of water.

"Great job," called Cragger. "If we weren't doomed before, now we really are."

"Just . . . stay there!" yelled Laval. "I'm coming!"

"Where do you think I'm going to go?" Cragger struggled against the ropes. "This thing makes one of Gorzan's hugs look like a bunny cuddle."

Laval was about to reply when, suddenly, he heard a loud groan behind him. He turned just in time to see the Gorilla statue tipping forward! Laval tried to spring out of the way, but he wasn't fast enough. The statue toppled on top of him.

"Oof!" the Lion exclaimed. The heavy statue pinned him to the ground.

"Laval! Are you okay?" Cragger called.

"Yeah, I think so," Laval said. "But I'm . . . LOOK OUT!"

Laval's eyes grew wide as a flame cannon went off beside Cragger. In an instant, the Croc was surrounded by flames!

"CRAGGER!" Laval cried.

For a moment, Laval couldn't see anything but embers and smoke. Then, he heard coughing. When the smoke cleared, Cragger was sputtering and waving his arms. Instead of hurting the Croc, the flames had burned right through the ropes tying him up. He was free!

"Talk about luck." Laval exhaled. "Are you hurt?"

"Just a little singed," said Cragger. "You?"

Laval squirmed under the statue. "Been better. Could use a little help here."

Cragger moved toward Laval. But as he did, the floor shook again. The whole room turned, and the stairs by the doorway reappeared. All Cragger had to do was make a run for it and he would be free! But the room could shift any minute and they would disappear again.

Cragger met Laval's gaze for a split second. Then he turned and ran.

"Cragger?" Laval's heart sank. The Crocodile wouldn't really leave him there?

Would he?

Suddenly, Cragger swerved and jumped over a marching group of Skunk mechs. He snatched a wrench from one of the mech's hands and skidded to a stop right beside Laval.

"Quick!" he said, using the wrench for leverage against the statue. "We'll push together—hurry!"

Together, the two managed to pry the Gorilla statue off of Laval. Cragger helped him to his feet. "Let's get out of here!" he shouted.

Running faster than they ever had before, they shot through the room and made it out the door just as the floor was starting to turn again.

Together, they clambered back up the stairs. When they got to the top, the Lion and Croc leaned heavily against the wall, gasping for breath.

"Thanks," Laval said finally. "For a second there, I wasn't sure you were going to come back for me."

Cragger shrugged and gave a big Crocodile grin. "We're friends, right? That's what friends do."

Laval smiled and clapped Cragger on the back. "It sure is."

A WEB OF WOOD

"**T**his place is *crazy*," said Gorzan as the group walked down a shadowy jungle path. "I've never seen plants like this before."

"Well, it gives me the creeps," said Worriz. "In case you didn't notice, we're boxed in on every side. We couldn't get off this road if we wanted to."

Worriz was right. Thick tangles of vines surrounded the warriors with broad leaves and dozens of long, sharp thorns on each strand.

The only one who seemed to be enjoying this part of the journey was Rogon's Rhinoceros Legend Beast. He happily trudged along, sniffing leaves as they went.

The friends had saved the Rhinoceros Legend Beast from the Outland Tribes a few days before. Now, the Beast was joining them on their journey. As the heroes continued through the jungle, the great Rhino discovered that the green leaves on the vines tasted really good. So he kept lagging behind to munch on them.

Suddenly, Eris swooped down from above. She had been scouting the path ahead for danger. "Oh, Laval, we've got trouble!" she called.

"What now?" groaned Cragger. "Bats? Scorpions? Pits of flame? Toxic mud creatures forty feet high?"

"I think you have to see it to believe it," said Eris. "Go around the bend. You can't miss it."

Laval and the group did as she said. When they rounded the corner, they stopped and stared. A few of them rubbed their eyes to make sure they weren't seeing things.

Looming in front of them was an enormous Spider Web unlike anything they had ever seen. It was as wide as the jungle path and rose at least sixty feet into the air. But it wasn't made out of Spider silk—it was made out of wood! The Spiders had meticulously constructed the towering web out of thick tree trunks, locking them together to form an impassable blockade.

"It's a barrier," said Laval, "and I'm not sure how we can get through it."

"Why go through when we can go over?" asked Razar.

"He's right," said Eris. "Razar and I can fly above it. Maybe together we can carry the rest of you, one by one."

Laval took a few steps back and peered up at the web. Yes, it wasn't so high that the Eagle and Raven couldn't make it over. The top part did look kind of strange, though. In the upper sections of the web, there were rows and rows of smaller tree limbs with sharpened ends. All of them were lined up so that their points faced the sky.

"What do you think, Worriz?" asked Laval.

The Wolf frowned. He didn't know much about Spiders or their webs, but he did know a lot about traps. This thing gave him a bad feeling. "I think it can't be that easy," Worriz replied. "But if those two want to try it, let 'em. I don't have any better ideas."

Laval looked at Eris and nodded once. She immediately shot up into the sky, soaring toward the top of the web. Just as she started to pass over it, one of the sharpened tree limbs shot out at her! Eris screeched in surprise and just barely managed to dodge it.

A second one grazed her wing and almost knocked her out of the sky. Shaken, she flew back to the ground.

"Wow," Eris said, shaking her head. "That thing is dangerous!"

Bladvic the Bear opened his sleepy eyes. "Knock it down," he said through a yawn.

"Right, and how do we do that without bringing it down on our heads?" asked Laval.

But the Bear had fallen back to sleep again. Laval didn't bother to wake him. The answer was obvious: There was no way to bring the web down without risking everyone being crushed. Even trying to carefully take it apart would be risky—one wrong move and the whole thing could crash to the ground.

"Maybe we could dig a tunnel and go underneath it?" suggested Eris.

"It would have to be an awfully huge tunnel," said Cragger. "Rogon's Legend Beast isn't exactly slim . . . and with the way he's eating those leaves, he's just going to get bigger."

"How about climbing it?" asked Gorzan. "I could go first, since I'm the best climber. Might be a groovy experience."

"Or your last," said Worriz. "What we need is someone who knows all about Spiders and their webs."

"Ha! The thing is simplicity itself!"

Everybody turned around at once. The words had come from Rogon. His whole expression had changed from dull and friendly to confident and brilliant. His eyes gleamed and his mouth curled into a knowing smile.

"Oh, here we go again," sighed Worriz.

Ever since they had freed Rogon's Legend Beast, something odd had been happening. Whenever the Legend Beast got close to Rogon, the young Rhino suddenly went from not too bright to incredibly smart.

But if the Legend Beast wandered away, Rogon would go back to his old self.

"Hey, if he has an idea, I want to hear it," said Laval.

"An idea?" said Rogon. "Why, it's so easy a calf could figure it out."

"Great," said Worriz. "Let's find a calf and ask him, then."

"No, let's give him a chance," said Laval. "Rogon, do you know a way to take the web apart?"

"Naturally," said Rogon. "You can take it apart quite easily . . . from the other side."

"Well, that's a lot of help," grumbled Worriz. "Got any more good news?"

Rogon chuckled. "Oh, my Wolfish friend, how amusing. The answer to our problem is obvious to anyone who understands Spider methods of construction. It's all about safe strands, you see."

"Safe strands?" asked Cragger. "What are those?"

Rogon looked over his shoulder, then back at the Crocodile. "Um, I don't know. Is this a test? I didn't know we were having a test today."

"The Legend Beast wandered away again," growled Laval. "Somebody go get him back."

"I'll go," said Worriz. The Wolf ran off. Most of the leaves near where the team was standing had been eaten, so Worriz guessed the Legend Beast had gone back down the path looking for any he had missed. Sure enough, that was where he found the great creature. It only took a little gentle persuasion to get him heading in the right direction.

Once the Legend Beast was back with the group, Rogon's manner abruptly changed.

"Now, where was I? Oh, yes, safe strands . . . When a Spider builds a web, he can't very well make it so that he himself will get stuck when walking on it, right?"

"That makes sense," agreed Laval.

"So, some strands are not sticky," explained Rogon. "They are safe for the Spider to walk on."

"Hey, I see it now," said Gorzan. "There must be some pieces of that web that are safe for us to climb on. Those are the ones the Spiders used when they were building it. If we can figure out which ones they are, we can make it through."

"What about the Legend Beast?" asked Eris. "He can't climb."

"Never fear, my avian ally," said Rogon. "I have ideas about that, too. But first . . ."

Rogon stood very still and stared at the web for a few minutes. Then he nodded. "Yes. Oh, how interesting, a fine piece of work indeed. There is a precise mathematical pattern to the placement of the pieces. Using that knowledge, I can safely chart our course through the web. Follow me!"

One by one, the travelers started to climb up the giant wooden structure. Rogon patiently led them, moving carefully from tree trunk to tree trunk. Everyone had been warned to do exactly what he did. "A single misstep,"

Rogon reminded them, "and we will end up at the bottom of a very large woodpile."

They had made it about halfway through the web when Rogon stopped. *"Hmmmm,"* he said.

"Hmmmm, what?" asked Laval. "Is that a good *hmmmm* or a bad *hmmmm*?"

"The pattern has been altered," said Rogon. "They changed something . . . let me see . . . oh, yes, I see it now, it's . . . it's . . ."

"What?" Laval asked loudly.

"Wow, it's cool up here," Rogon answered. "But how do we get down?"

Laval slapped a hand to his forehead. Cragger would have beaten his head against one of the tree trunks if he knew which ones were safe. Instead, Laval said, "Worriz. Legend Beast. Now."

Grumbling, the Wolf retraced his path and went to find the Legend Beast. Meanwhile, the wait had made Bladvic doze off again. His head started to droop, and he slumped against one of the pieces of the web. Eris spotted what was happening and lunged at him, struggling to lift his head off the tree trunk.

"He hit the wrong piece!" she shouted as the others nearby helped her prop up the Bear.

But it was too late. The web was already starting to teeter. High above, pieces were rocking with enough force to disconnect from one another.

"Let's go!" said Cragger. "What difference does it make how we get over now as long as we make it over?"

"Wait, there's still a chance, if Worriz brings back the Legend Beast," said Laval. "Hang on!"

They could see Worriz in the distance. But the huge Rhino behind him kept stopping to snack on the few leaves he could spot. Worriz looked back in frustration.

Too bad that web doesn't have leaves, the Wolf thought. *Hey, wait a minute . . .*

Moving as fast as he could, Worriz raced back and forth down the trail, gathering as many leaves as he could. Once he had a large armful, he ran back toward the web.

The Legend Beast picked up the scent of his new favorite food and followed.

By the time Worriz reached the web the Legend Beast was close enough for Rogon to become smart again.

"Drop the leaves and get up here," Razar yelled.

"He'll eat them all in a couple of seconds and wander off again," Worriz replied. "We need to keep him close to Rogon."

Arms full of leaves, Worriz somehow managed to climb back up to where he had been. Fortunately, being a Wolf, his nose was sensitive enough to follow the scent of his companions across the right pieces of the web.

"See? It's working!" said Worriz. "He's not wandering away!"

"Indeed," said Rogon. "But it is perhaps too successful of a plan. Look!"

Worriz glanced down. The hungry Legend Beast *really* wanted the leaves Worriz was carrying and was trying to climb the web himself!

"Go! Go! Go!" Laval yelled at Rogon.

Rogon climbed as fast as he could, his amazing brain able to spot every change in the pattern that the Spiders had built into the web. The others raced along behind him, being careful to step where he stepped even as the web shook all around them.

"Success!" yelled Rogon as he made it safely over to the other side of the web. He climbed down about halfway and then jumped toward the ground, rolling for a long way before coming to a stop. Laval and the rest followed after him, but there was no time to celebrate.

The web was still in danger of collapsing on the Legend Beast.

"Rogon," said Laval, "we need to take this thing down! Can you do it?"

The Rhino nodded and said, "Yes, I see the key. There had to be a way the Spiders could dismantle this, and what they can do, we can do! But we'd better do it fast."

"I know!" cried Laval as one of the tree limbs tumbled off the web, crashing beside him. "Tell us what to do!"

Rogon explained, "Our resident masters of aviation must help us disassemble the ingenious contraption from an elevated level while we un-winged companions assist from our terrestrial positions."

The others looked at him in complete confusion. *"What?!"* they cried together.

Rogon smiled. "The spikes at the top only point the other way. They are no longer a threat to our winged allies. Eris and Razar must fly up and drop us the logs one by one."

Quickly, the Eagle and Raven shot up into the sky. But on the other side, the Rhino Legend Beast was becoming very frustrated that he couldn't get to the leaves Worriz was holding. He started to grunt and snort, nudging at the web with his giant horn. The entire web teetered.

"He's going to collapse it!" cried Laval.

Razar called down to Worriz. "My friend, you must keep the Beast distracted while we do our part, or we are all doomed."

"He's right!" exclaimed Eris. "Worriz, run back and forth so the Legend Beast chases after you instead of trying to break through the web. That will give us time to take it apart."

"You want me to do *what*?" exclaimed Worriz. "*Uggh*. Fine. But just watch where you're dropping those logs. Remember, I'm the only thing keeping that Beast from bringing down the whole web on top of us all."

Grumbling loudly, Worriz began running back and forth on his side of the web. He held out the leaves in plain sight for the Legend Beast to see.

The plan worked. The Legend Beast chased after him to the right edge of the web . . . then to the left . . . then back again. The ground trembled with its thundering footsteps. But at least it wasn't trying to collapse the web.

Swiftly, Razar and Eris dismantled the tottering contraption piece by piece from the top. Each time they pulled off a new log they would drop it down to their friends below. They followed Rogon's instructions exactly on which pieces to pull out next.

Soon, the heroes were surrounded by piles and piles of wood. But there was no more web.

The Legend Beast happily lumbered over the dismantled branches and began munching on the leaves Worriz was holding.

"That was a close one." Laval breathed a sigh of relief. "Thanks, Rogon. Without you, we would have been goners."

"Hey, what about me?" complained Worriz. "I was the one who got that Legend Beast close enough to keep Rogon smart, *and* I'm the one who distracted it while you took that giant web apart. Where's my thanks?"

Just then, the Legend Beast sniffed Worriz. The tasty scent of leaves still lingered on the Wolf's fur. The Legend Beast gave Worriz a great big lick.

"It seems you have your thanks, my friend," said Razar.

"Yeah." Laval chuckled. "As long as you smell like those leaves, that Legend Beast won't be wandering away from us anymore."

Worriz groaned as the Legend Beast licked him again. "Some thanks."

Everyone laughed.